I0520690

MILES LEDOUX

RING AROUND THE ROSIE

Winter in Veil, Book 4

First published by ABCs 2025

First edition

ISBN: 978-1-882508-84-6

Cover art by Rachel Kelli
Editing by Julie Mianecki

This book was professionally typeset on Reedsy.
Find out more at reedsy.com

Preface

Ring around the rosies
  A pocket full of posies
  Ashes, ashes
  We all fall down!

I

"Mmeep."

Sitting up in bed and gazing out the window, Violet stroked the calico cat curled up in her lap. Having finally gotten used to the house's new occupant, Roswell had been generous with his cuddles the past several days. His furry body thrummed warmly against her.

Outside, the sky was filled with falling snow. A week into November, this was Veil's first heavy snowfall of the season. Already, everything Violet could see from her window was buried in white. A gentle stirring of wind made the snowflakes dance. Part of her wanted to throw on some snow pants and go dance in it, herself, but a greater part of her was weighed down by sadness and lingering horror. She felt like nothing could cheer her up.

"Mmmeeep."

Almost nothing. She scratched the kitty's head behind his ears. He looked into her eyes and blinked appreciatively. "Mmmeep."

"Say, meee-yow."

"Mmeep."

"Yow. Meee*yow.*"

"Meep."

"Yeah, I used to try that," said a voice. "He's too stubborn."

1

Violet looked up as Cy entered carrying a tray with a bowl of noodle soup and some crackers. "Oh, don't worry about that," Cy told her as Violet hurried to put a face mask on. "You're not contagious anymore."

Violet's movement prompted the cat to hop off her bed and up to the windowsill beside her. Cy set the tray in the spot he had vacated.

"I've been meaning to ask you," said Violet, "I thought all calico cats are female."

"Oh, they are."

"Then how...?" Violet gestured at Roswell.

Cy shrugged. "From another planet?"

"Ohh. That explains the name."

Some soup had splashed onto Cy's hand. She reached for the tissue box at the head of the bed but found it empty. She noted all of the box's former contents crumpled and disposed of in the wastebasket. "Oh, Vi..."

Violet looked up, the soup spoon halfway to her mouth. "What?"

Cy gave her a sad, sympathetic smile. "Your nose isn't running that badly anymore." She nodded at the wastebasket. "You've been crying."

Violet set the spoon down dejectedly. "It's about the only thing I've been able to do, being stuck in bed all week."

"You need to give Mom and the other deputies more time. They'll figure out what happened."

"You mean who did it?" A smidgen of anger crept into Violet's voice.

Cy glanced down uncomfortably.

Violet went on, "When Deputy Benno got stuck in his search for Rob Mulroy, he took me to the last place Rob was seen. I didn't think I could be much help, but thanks to this weird, perfect memory of mine, I led him to a clue that *nobody* else could have seen. If I could get to the playground where they found Marcy, who knows what I could turn up?"

Cy steadied the soup bowl as Violet's movements caused it to slide toward the edge of the tray. "I already promised to take you there as soon as you're well."

"Why can't we go now? You just said I'm not contagious."

"Y-yes. But I also promised Mom and the nice doctors that I wouldn't take you out on an investigation while you're still recovering."

"Why would you promise that?!"

"Well, to be fair, the last time I did that, we got stranded in the middle of nowhere."

"That's not... Okay, yeah, that's fair." Grumpily, she ate a spoonful of soup.

"Listen," said Cy after a moment. "You're not the only one who wants to know...who killed her. I didn't know her too well, but Marcy had a lot of friends here in Veil. Some of my classmates did a vigil for her."

"I wish I could've gone," said Violet. "I know I only knew her for a few days, but..." Her eyes watered. Cy handed her a napkin. After drying her eyes, Violet went on, "I just... Since I woke up here—no memories of my past, no idea who I am—I've felt like...maybe there's a *reason* this happened to me. Maybe there's something I'm supposed to *do*. At any rate, having lost who I am, I think there *ought* to be a reason."

"Well, I think you've made a few big differences already."

"Not really for the better."

Cy gave her an incredulous stare. "You're kidding, right? First thing you did was scare the living crap out of my ex-boyfriend when he tried to assault me. Then you helped find a missing girl."

"Your mother would've found her anyway."

"On Halloween night you saved me from those guys trying to rob Pressler!"

"Myrna Redpath and your mom saved you. I just made things worse."

"You, um…met Candy. You helped her solve her problem."

"And then I drove her out of town."

Cy gave an exasperated sigh.

Violet looked down morosely. "Even if I help find Marcy's killer, it won't bring her back."

"No, it won't." The new voice made Cy and Violet look up. Jen stood in the doorway, in uniform. "But when we catch him, we'll make sure he doesn't hurt anybody else."

Violet gave a grim smile.

Jen asked Cy, "How's she doing?"

"She's crazy."

Violet groaned. "Don't you have school?"

"Nope. Canceled. You're stuck with me."

"Mmmeep."

"And him."

"Did you clean his litter box?" asked Jen.

In response, Cy said, "Be right back."

Alone with Violet, Jen told her, "As soon as we come up with anything in the case of Marcy's murder, I'll let you know."

"Isn't there a rule against that?"

Jen shrugged. "I won't tell if you won't."

Quietly Violet said, "Thanks."

Jen turned to leave. Just short of the doorway, she looked back and paused. Violet was looking out the window again.

She wore a pinched expression—not squinting exactly, but she seemed to be straining in some way. "Violet?"

"Yeah?"

Jen came back into the room. "Is something else bothering you?"

Violet seemed flustered. "What do you mean? Why—why would something else be bothering me?"

"I don't know. You tell me." Jen gave her a sideways look.

Violet turned her head away, to face the window again. A few awkward seconds passed, then: "Okay, there is something. It's probably not important, but..."

"What is it?"

Violet turned back to her. "You know the neighbors?"

"The Dosleys?" They were the only people who lived close enough to be considered neighbors.

"I mean, if the schools are canceled, most businesses probably are, too. It's just, they normally have this set routine—one car leaves at seven-thirty, the other leaves about an hour later. And there are other things—I don't know what they are, but the sounds are the same every morning. Today I haven't even heard their garage door open yet. I guess when you remember everything all the time, even when you're not trying, you get sensitive to little things, patterns that get broken. So, like I said, it's probably not important—"

"Violet." The look Jen gave her was stern but amused. "Would it make you feel better if I checked on our neighbors?"

Violet let out an embarrassed laugh.

In her heavy-duty boots Jen tromped through the snow across the fifty meters that separated the two houses. Feeling the snow crunching beneath her feet reminded her of the joyous times she'd had playing in it as a child. The people of this area might have fallen short of making Jen feel safe and belonging, but the area itself had always felt welcoming.

She first suspected trouble when she sighted the Dosleys' front door standing ajar.

It was a two-story house, its light blue walls just showing through the thickening snow in ragged horizontal stripes. A two-car garage of the same color sat next to it. Someone had shoveled the driveway recently. Perhaps that someone had forgotten to close the door when they went inside.

Jen trotted up to the front door and knocked. "Hello? Hello! It's Jen Grogan from next door. Is anyone home?" An eerie silence answered her. Carefully she pushed the door the rest of the way open. Just inside was a plethora of coats and boots clumped together on a bench and on the floor. One pair of boots still bore some unmelted snow.

"Joy? Fran?" Jen took a step inside. "Kristy? Are you guys okay?"

A moment after the fact, she felt her hand hovering near her sidearm.

There were no lights on in the living room. At the far end of the central hallway, lights appeared to be lit in the kitchen. Jen crept warily in that direction. Halfway down the hall, she thought she heard a noise in the living room, but when she took another look, she saw no one.

In the kitchen, the table was laid out for breakfast, though the meal had already been partially eaten. One plate had even made it as far as the sink.

Jen's fingers brushed the handle of her sidearm. "To anyone who can hear me," she said in a clear, no-nonsense voice, "I'm Deputy Grogan of the Veil sheriff's department. If you belong in this house, please say something so I can help you." She paced slowly through the living room, back toward the front of the house. "If you *don't* belong here, you need to make your presence known *now*."

She waited.

All at once she heard a scream.

It came from upstairs. Jen tore up the steps, all the while hearing more screams, louder, growing in intensity.

By the time she burst through the door at the top, her weapon was out. Quickly she scanned the room—and right away spotted the source of the screams—

It was a baby.

A three, maybe four-month-old baby lying in a crib. Big, brightly colored letters on the nursery wall spelled out *ROSIE*.

But the baby wasn't the only occupant of the room. Lying on the floor beside the crib was a figure with long blond hair and an oversized shirt. It wasn't moving.

"Oh my god, Kristy!" Jen swooped down beside the seventeen-year-old girl. Her face felt clammy. Jen rolled her onto her back and put her ear to the girl's face. Her breath was faint.

Jen clicked her radio. "Officer calling dispatch! I need an ambulance at seven-eighteen Old Route Nine! And send backup!"

As she kept trying to rouse the girl, the baby continued to scream.

II

"**N**o, sir," said Jen's voice over the radio. *"So far they haven't found any trace of the parents, Fran or Joy."*

"What do you mean, 'they?'" replied the sheriff, sitting in his office. "Aren't you leading the search?"

"Well, sir, I'd really love to, but apparently I'm the only deputy who isn't 'not good with babies,' so Rosie's here at my house."

"Oh, for crying out loud."

"What's the ETA on the caretaker from social services?"

"It's...not definite."

"Ah. The snow?"

"Exactly. All the surrounding roads are blocked. Can you hold out for a while?"

"I can handle a baby, sir. I'm just very anxious to find out what happened to the Dosleys. They're good people." That wasn't something Jen often said about the residents of her hometown.

"Well, the hospital tells me Kristy had some sort of drug in her system. A common date rape drug, apparently."

"Was she...?"

"She's physically fine otherwise."

"Thank God. But then, what, did they knock out the daughter in order to kidnap the parents?"

"If there was an outsider vehicle at that place, there would have been tire tracks leading in and out of the driveway," said the sheriff, a question in his tone.

"That's right—and there weren't."

"Are you sure?"

"Positive. And both cars are still in the garage."

"Could the parents have left on their own? On foot?"

"Hm. I don't know. I'll have to take another look." A shrill wail made the sheriff wince and pull his ear away from the phone. *"Darn it. I thought I'd gotten her to sleep."*

"I'll tell Deputy Derrick to sweep the house again. The parents have gotta be there."

The crying stopped. *"There you go,"* said Jen in a distinctly less formal tone of voice. *"Yeah, you like that, huh! That's yummy! Oh, uh, thank you, sir."*

"No worries. And tell the kid her big sister'll be fine."

"Her sister?"

"Yes. Kristy."

"Sir...Kristy is the baby's mother."

"Oh...right."

* * *

Perseus, what's going on? signed the young woman on the phone screen. *I thought you were excited about me coming to visit.*

I am, Benno signed in return. *I can't wait to see you, but now is not a good time.*

I bet you met someone. You don't want me being a third wheel.

No, I haven't, Benno insisted. *It doesn't have to do with me. It's to do with work.*

You're putting me off for work?!

No! I'm trying to... I'm trying to keep you safe.

The woman's expression turned from playful to serious. *Perseus, are you in trouble?*

Pam, I really can't tell you more than that.

So you're in trouble.

Benno rolled his eyes. *And this is why I didn't want to talk to you about it! Whenever I'm trying to keep a secret, you always press me and I say more than I'm supposed to!*

The landline began to ring.

This is the call I've been waiting for. Pam, I'll call you back.

But—

I love you! His sister's anxious, scowling face disappeared from his phone screen before he answered the landline. "Hello, Veil sheriff's department. Deputy Benno speaking."

Ten minutes and many scribbled notes later, he entered the sheriff's office and closed the door.

"Four mysterious deaths," the sheriff repeated musingly after Benno had given his report.

"Three of them within forty miles, the other, sixty. All within the past eighteen months," Benno confirmed. "And all technically ruled as accidental."

"Technically?"

"Well, based on the limited evidence in each case, there was no other choice. But all of the investigators were dissatisfied. They felt like there was too much left unexplained. They closed the cases only because there wasn't enough to build upon."

The sheriff nodded to himself. "Just like we would've closed the case on Mulroy, if there had been one. And Foley, too." He shook his head in puzzlement. "But why not Marcy Temple? Why hide the other two bodies but not hers? Why not cover up this last murder like they did the others?" He let out a short, humorless laugh. "That is, assuming she was killed by the same person. Maybe we have *two* killers in Veil. Or three even—one for each victim—and it's not a serial killer at all." He pressed his hands over his face. "We're gonna have a panic on our hands," he said in a falsely cheery voice.

Benno was frowning. "I don't know, sir. I have a gut feeling it's the same killer for all three."

"Well, the first two, maybe. Thanks to the blood and DNA we found on the bridge, we know where and approximately when Foley was killed. That means both victims were ambushed at night, alone—or almost alone, in Mulroy's case. The murders were planned, premeditated, the bodies removed afterward. That's too many coincidences to swallow for there to be two different killers. But the third murder…"

"Actually, sir, if there are two killers, I'd say it's more likely the Mulroy murder is the odd one out."

The sheriff leaned back with raised eyebrows. "Now, why do you say that, Deputy?"

"Well, first, the recording implies that *that* murder has something to do with the amnesiac, Violet."

"*Pos*sibly," the sheriff said guardedly. "But then why didn't the shooter also kill Tuck Fleagle? Besides which, Fleagle is clearly drunk on the recording, and I've heard enough about him not to trust him as a source of information."

"Yes, sir." Benno looked crestfallen.

"Not that we shouldn't keep trying to find him, of course. We need him as a material witness. And even if Violet *is* involved, she won't be any help to us unless she gets her memories back." The sheriff got up and circled the desk to stand next to the deputy. "What about the other two murders? Any possible connection between them?"

"Well, sir, both of the victims were at the pagan sabbat about two weeks ago. Also, both murders seemed…staged. After Marcy Temple was killed, the murderer rolled her onto her back, opened her eyes, and sprinkled dirt over her face for some reason. And even though we didn't find Foley's body—do you remember where I found the murder weapon?"

"That wooden club? You said it was stuck in the bridge."

"Right. But the murderer could've disposed of it in any number of ways—left it in the middle of the woods, driven out of town and tossed it out a window... Instead he left it right where he committed the murder."

"You said you only found the club because you stumbled onto a lead by chance. Without it, we wouldn't have even examined the bridge."

"Yes, I know, sir, but..."

"But," the sheriff picked up the thought, "what if we *were* meant to find the club—just not this soon?"

Slowly they both grinned. "I hadn't thought of that, sir," said Benno.

The sheriff put a hand on his shoulder. "Keep digging into those deaths in other parts of Vermont," he said conspiratorially, "but be discreet. If we're not supposed to know about a series of murders, then let's not tip our hand."

"Yes, sir." Benno moved toward the door, turned back to say something, then hesitated.

"What is it, Benno?"

"Sir...on the off-chance that Mulroy's death *does* have something to do with Violet, shouldn't we warn Jen—I mean, Deputy Grogan? If the murderer comes after Violet and she's staying with—"

"Deputy," the sheriff said sternly, "we've been through this. If and when we find Rob Mulroy's corpse with a bullet hole in it, Jen Grogan officially becomes the prime suspect. She's the only one we know of with a strong motive—besides her own *daughter*. If we involve her in the investigation beforehand, we shoot ourselves in the foot."

"But she was—"

"Even if she was the one who asked you to look into Mulroy's disappearance in the first place." More gently he said, "I know you hate keeping things from her, Benno—believe me, it's reassuring to me to know you do. But this is the way it's gotta be."

"Yes, sir," Benno said resignedly. He turned to leave.

"Oh, one more thing, Deputy." The sheriff circled back to his chair. "That wasn't dirt sprinkled on Marcy Temple's face."

"What was it, sir?"

"Pepper."

"Pepper, sir?"

"According to the lab, yeah."

Benno exited but stood for a moment on the other side of the closed door, frowning pensively. He mouthed the word *pepper* to himself, and then again.

* * *

"This house isn't that big!" Deputy James Derrick griped as he climbed back up the stairs from the Dosleys' basement. "There can't be that many places for two women to hide!"

Deputy Debbie Tan climbed up on a chair to examine the windows over the sink. "They're probably dead," she said, deadpan.

Deputy Jessica Hayden popped her head up from behind the kitchen island. "Debbie, come on," she said. "One pessimist is enough." Her eyes darted toward Derrick.

"It's not pessimism," said Tan. "If the Dosleys are still in the house, they must be hidden in places we haven't thought to look in. Places smaller than you'd expect somebody to be able to fit into. Right after someone dies, before rigor mortis sets in, you can get people into really tight spaces because their muscles are more relaxed than they've ever been." She pointed at Derrick. "If you died right now, I could fit you into that cupboard under the sink." She looked again at the cupboard, then glanced back at Hayden. "Heck, I could fit both of you."

Hayden glanced downward at her stocky frame and eyed Tan skeptically.

"None of the ground-floor windows has been tampered with," Tan went on casually, hopping down from the chair. "I'll check upstairs."

Once Tan was out of earshot, Derrick asked Hayden, "Is she always this morbid?"

"What, that? That was nothing. If you ever want help going vegan, have lunch with her." Hayden headed for the living room.

Left alone in the kitchen, Derrick turned on the spot, uncertain where to search next. His eyes soon fell on the door to the cupboard under the sink. He made a face, started to move away, then halted, doubled back and, making sure his fellow deputies were fully occupied elsewhere, he tugged on the door with his foot…

"Deputy Derrick!"

Startled, he nearly lost his balance and fell over. "What?!"

"You should have a look at this."

He stomped out to the living room.

A few seconds after he left, a pair of eyes rose up outside the glass in the back door. Satisfied the kitchen was vacant, Cy eased the door open, came inside, then shut it just as quietly behind her. She surveyed the room briefly, then pulled out her phone and started taking pictures.

As he examined the papers Hayden was showing him, Deputy

Derrick pulled out his own phone when it rang, and he answered, "Hello?"

"It's Grogan. What've you got for me?"

The last time Jen had called Deputy Derrick was on Halloween. That time, he had been rude and insubordinate (as senior deputy, she was technically his superior). This had turned out to be a grave mistake on his part. Today, resentful as he might feel about her running the investigation from next door, he kept it completely hidden. "We're going over the house for the second time. There's no sign of the Dosleys or any intruders."

He heard Jen exhale heavily. *"I see."*

"But we did come across some legal documents—"

"A-*hem.*" Deputy Hayden glared at him.

"*Hayden* found some legal documents that might have some bearing on the case."

"Send them over."

"Yes, ma'am."

Deputy Tan came back downstairs as he hung up. "No one's entered from outside on the second floor," she reported.

Derrick threw up his hands. "No one's entered, no one's left. We can search through the garage one more time, but if we still don't find anything, I don't know what to do next. Where else can we search?!"

Tan shrugged. "Maybe we should ask the girl sneaking down the hall."

There was the sound of sharp movement, followed by a *thump* and an "Ow!"

Deputy Derrick let out a growl.

Cy appeared from around the corner, rubbing her elbow and grimacing. "Okay, so, before you get mad—"

"*Cyanne!*"

She winced. "Too late."

"You can't keep interfering in our investigations! Being a deputy's kid does not give you special privilege! If you want to actually be a deputy, you have to put in the time and the work, you can't just waltz in like an amateur P.I.!"

Cy regarded him with a glazed expression.

Incensed, Derrick took a step toward her. "Are you even listening to me?!"

She counted on her fingers. "No interfering, no special privilege. Got it."

"No," said Derrick, shaking his head, "no, you say that, but then you're just gonna turn around and do it again. What, do I need to arrest you?"

Cy gave him a quizzical look. "I don't think you can do that."

Deputy Derrick looked very tempted to prove her wrong, but Tan interjected, "You could threaten to tell her mother."

Cy's jaw dropped. "Dude!"

Raising and lowering his hand in a show of containing his temper, Derrick snapped, "Everyone, quiet! Hayden, escort this kid back home. And give these to Deputy Grogan." He thrust the legal documents at her.

As Hayden led her down the hall toward the front door, Cy asked, "Is he ever not in a bad mood?"

Hayden automatically answered, "No."

Derrick stood in the living room, waiting for the sound of the door opening and then closing behind the interloper. Instead he heard Cy give a yelp, then something heavy falling over. Then he heard Cy give a cry of alarm. "No!" he snapped, striding through the living room toward the front door. "No more stalling! I want you out—" He entered the hall and froze.

16

Cy had tripped over a boot amid the mass of outdoor clothes piled near the door. The boot proved to be part of a larger mass that flopped over, separating from the pile. Derrick stared in amazement at the small, unconscious woman in her late forties with one arm inside a long overcoat, which until now had hidden her from sight.

"Joy!" exclaimed Cy. "It's Joy Dosley!" She knelt beside her, shook her. "Joy, can you hear me? Wake up! Joy! *Joy!*"

III

Again, the ambulance had come and gone. As soon as Violet heard it, she ran in her slipper-clad feet, bathrobe swishing, down the hall to the window over the front staircase. There she craned her neck to the right, watching the flashing red lights approach from the direction of town, listening as Jen, at the bottom of the stairs, called her deputies back and demanded to know what was going on. Apparently another of the Dosley family had been found unconscious, just like the girl, Kristy. Any other details that might have been forthcoming were lost when the sirens woke up Rosie, and Jen went to take care of her.

Now Violet stood peering out the window in the upstairs laundry room, gazing at the house next door surrounded by patrol cars, all gradually disappearing under a layer of snow. She wasn't actually tall enough to see out the window, so she stood on the bottom lip of the laundry chute that descended from the floor above, bracing herself with one hand on the shelf over the washer. Violet wondered what the deputies were doing there now, how they were going about the investigation. Who had drugged the neighbors, and why? How had the culprit gotten in and out of the house without leaving a trace? And where was the last Dosley?

Once again Violet felt that itch, that yearning to investigate, to unravel a mystery. Wanting to track down Marcy's killer had fueled that desire, of course, but she admitted to herself that the instinct ran deeper, that it had awakened the moment she'd had her epiphany on Halloween night. Deputy Benno had asked her to help him find a lead in the case of a missing man, had brought her to the man's last known location. There she'd stood, reached down into the depths of her own confused, chaotic memories, and plucked out the very one they'd needed. It hadn't been easy—Violet had had to take the time to familiarize herself with the workings of her own mind—but the results had brought such a feeling of satisfaction, of…of fulfillment. Over the next few days she'd become more and more certain: this was what she was meant for.

She stepped down from the chute and took a breath. Her lungs felt clear. All of her felt fine and healthy. Why did she have to stay cooped up in this house? She was ready to help—to solve the mystery of the missing man, the mystery of the Dosleys, the mystery of Marcy's murder—

And stop it from happening ever again, she thought, *to anyone else.*

At that thought, she went completely still, barely breathing. She didn't move for several seconds, didn't react to the sound of knocking downstairs. Cy's voice sounded harried as she opened the front door and said, "Can I help you?"

Violet bolted for the bathroom. She made it to the toilet just in time before she threw up.

* * *

Jen hadn't seemed too angry when she learned that Cy had snuck into the Dosleys' house during the investigation. Since Halloween, both of them had tried extra-hard to keep their tempers in check when interacting with each other. She had even looked impressed when Cy explained that she'd been trying to *help* with the investigation. Nevertheless, there were consequences for breaking rules.

"Next, place the new diaper directly under the wet diaper. This will prevent messes from spreading. Then take off the wet diaper..."

Cy followed along with the YouTube video on her laptop, pausing it occasionally. She'd changed babies' diapers before but wanted to make sure she wasn't forgetting anything. "Aagh! Rosie, no!" After taking it off, she'd placed the soiled diaper too close, and Rosie's kicking feet had found it.

Cy had barely finished the task and disposed of the mess when there was a knock at the front door. Hoisting the baby into her left arm, she answered it. "Can I help you?"

A tall, thin woman in her fifties stood on the front porch, a canvas bag hanging from one shoulder. Long, silvery black hair ran down her back. Her cheeks were rosy, probably from the cold. "Um, hi, excuse me," she said, a little flustered. "Do you know what's happening next door, with all those police officers?"

"Well, technically they're sheriff's deputies, but—"

"Wait, is that Rosie?" The woman pointed at the baby, then waved, her eyes and mouth opening up wide. "Hi, Rosie! Hi!" she cooed, her voice going up an octave.

"How do you know Rosie?"

"I'm her nanny!"

"Her nanny?!"

"Yes, I live just up the road. My name's Rita Brandt. I come and help out with the baby a few times a week. What's she doing here?"

"A nanny..." Cy looked as if Christmas had come early. "Come inside," she said. Hastily she explained the situation. Rita was especially concerned that Fran Dosley had not yet been found.

"So, you said your mother is in charge of the investigation," Rita clarified. "Is she here?"

"No, she's gone to interview Rosie's father," said Cy. "Come on, this way. All of Rosie's stuff is back here." She led Rita through the dining room and into the kitchen, where Deputy Hayden was leaning out the back door.

"Cy!!" called the deputy.

"Right here."

The deputy closed the door with a huff. "Cy, please don't take the baby outside."

Cy gave her a strange look. "Outside? No, I just answered the door. I didn't go outside."

"You didn't?" Hayden looked back and forth between Cy and the back door in confusion.

"No, I didn't. Also, I'm off baby duty. This is Rita, Rosie's nanny."

Most of the baby equipment they'd found in the Dosleys' house had been laid on the kitchen table and its benches. Rita showed familiarity with it at once and, taking Rosie off Cy's hands, set about feeding her.

"How long have you been their nanny?" asked Deputy Hayden.

"Two months," said Rita. "Poor Kristy is trying hard to keep up with her education, get her GED, and her parents both have to work, so I've been helping out."

Cy, just then mixing a glass of Tang to bring up to Violet, felt a pang of guilt. She'd met Kristy shortly after she moved to Veil. The girl had been shy but pleasant—and very pregnant at the time. Cy's mother had tried to persuade her to hang out with Kristy, to start forming a local circle of friends. But at that point, deep in her resentment and determination not to do anything her mother wanted, she'd outright refused. It hadn't even occurred to her at the time that maybe Kristy *needed* a friend. Swallowing her regret, Cy resolved to let Kristy know—once she woke up—that she was there for her.

"What do Kristy's parents do?" asked the deputy.

"Fran is a secretary at the school and Joy runs that little store on Main Street, with the natural foods."

Cy turned to her. "Do you have any idea who would do this to their family, or why?"

Rita shrugged. "I know the parents of Kristy's ex-boyfriend are suing the Dosleys so their son doesn't have to pay child support, but I never imagined they might try to *hurt* them."

That must be what the legal documents were about, thought Cy.

"They've never said or done anything threatening?" Hayden asked the nanny.

Rita shook her head. "They wouldn't do anything to draw more attention to the situation than they have to. The parents are embarrassed, and this is the only way they know to deal with it."

Rosie began babbling, her appetite apparently sated. Rita proceeded to burp her. Cy stared at the little round face and marveled that anyone would be embarrassed by her, diapers or no diapers. She left the room as Rita began singing the baby a nursery rhyme.

* * *

"'Pop Goes the Weasel?'"

Deputy Benno had never seen the sheriff's eyebrows rise so high. "Y-yes, sir. When you told me about the pepper on Marcy Temple's nose, it felt familiar to me. I thought maybe I'd heard

22

of another case where the murderer left that signature, but when I searched cases involving pepper, I drew a blank."

"Uh-huh…" The eyebrows were still high up.

"Then I remembered there's a line from the nursery rhyme, 'Pop Goes the Weasel.' It goes"—he was about to sing but then thought better of it and merely spoke the words—"'Put some pepper on his nose / And you'll make him sneeze-l'—"

"*Sneeze-l?*"

"It's just to make it rhyme, sir."

"Oh…"

"'Catch him fast before he snaps / Pop goes the weasel.'"

The sheriff nodded slowly. "And this is the only lead you've come up with."

"Well—"

"I thought 'Pop Goes the Weasel' had just the one verse."

"Actually it has at least ten."

The sheriff went bug-eyed for a moment. "I see. Well, that's interesting, Deputy, but—"

"Sir, the other deaths tie into the rhyme, too."

The eyebrows abruptly went down again. He leaned forward. "What do you mean?"

"Right before the line about the pepper, the previous verse is, 'Every night when I go out / The monkey's on the table / Take a stick and knock it off / Pop goes the weasel.'"

"That…doesn't rhyme."

"I know, sir, but—"

"And why are all nursery rhymes so violent? Instead of assaulting the monkey, you could just give him a banana. That's animal cruelty."

"Well, sir, it's actually slang."

"Slang?"

23

Benno glanced at his notes. "Yes, sir, the 'monkey,' in this case, refers to an alcoholic drink. To take a stick and knock it off means to—well, to drink it. But anyway," he hurried on, "Matt Foley, going by the physical evidence, was knocked off the bridge with—"

"The wooden club."

"A stick!"

Only one eyebrow went up this time.

"And I remember, some people in town referred to Foley as a *monkey*—probably in reference to the Scopes Monkey Trial, because of all his anti-religious rhetoric."

The sheriff sounded afraid to ask, even as he did so: "And Rob Mulroy?"

"Well, sir, the gunshot could be considered to be a very loud… *pop*."

"Mm-hm."

"I know it's thin, sir—"

"That's one word for it."

"But I rechecked the reports on the other mysterious deaths in Vermont from the past year and a half, and they all involve some slight reference to the song: one victim found near a statue of a golden eagle, another with a torn pair of pants—torn *post*-mortem—a ripped-up painting…"

"Deputy." The sheriff waved his hand in a cease-and-desist motion. "I want you to keep looking for connections in the *physical* evidence. All right?"

Benno held back a sigh. "Yes, sir."

"Like Mulroy's car—in the recording you found, he berates Fleagle for walking, which implies Mulroy drove. So why didn't we find his car at the scene?"

"Yes, sir."

"And I'll keep checking for connections between the victims, themselves."

"Yes, sir." Benno exited.

Dubowski reawakened his computer, about to keep working, but then he looked away, thinking to himself.

He opened the office door and called after Benno, "Just out of curiosity…what's the verse *after* the line about the pepper?"

"Oh!" For a moment Benno looked like a deer caught in headlights. "Well, apparently no one can agree on the exact order of the verses."

"Of course not."

"In one version, it's something about buying a pig, in another, it's about going to the grocery store—"

"All right, all right." The sheriff went back into his office.

* * *

It had been extremely close, Rita admitted to herself.

What on earth had possessed that deputy woman to visit her next-door neighbors at that exact moment?! Only providence and quick thinking had saved her. For a brief time, she'd lost all hope for her mission, but then that same deputy had returned to her house *with the baby*. There was still a chance of success.

Getting into the house next door without being seen had been a challenge, but she'd made it. Once there, she waited, listening from just inside the basement door, watching through the ground-level windows that faced the Dosley house. She saw the deputy's daughter sneak out, heard the deputy on the phone with her colleagues. She took the opportunity to slip upstairs and make some arrangements, then whisked back to her hiding place just as the daughter returned.

When Deputy Grogan finally left the house, leaving only the teenage daughter and the baby, Rita knew this was her chance.

Rather than try to ambush the daughter, she decided the wiser course of action would be to gain her trust—and *then* ambush her.

She could hear the daughter's computer giving a tutorial on how to change a diaper. With the girl distracted, Rita slipped out of the basement, tiptoed out the back door, and dashed around to the front. Then, brushing dust off herself, she strode up the porch steps and knocked.

The girl swallowed the nanny cover story without any misgivings. Once she set down the baby, she would be at Rita's mercy. Rita followed her into the kitchen, eyeing her up and down, sizing up her physical vulnerabilities and deciding which one to—

There, in the kitchen, was *another* deputy. Of course they wouldn't have left the baby without an adult guardian in the house. Inconvenient, but once more, fortune favored Rita: although the deputy had heard her leave through the back door, she'd assumed it was the teenager.

Again Rita would have to continue waiting, to keep up this role for a while longer—not too long, though. The Dosleys could expose her once they were able. The risks were great.

But her mission was too important to give up.

IV

The two glasses on the Dosleys' breakfast table were almost empty, one containing milk, the other, Tang. At the third place was a mug of tea that was half full.

"So," said Violet in her bedroom, examining the photos on Cy's phone, "Kristy was found upstairs next to the crib, and Joy was…"

"Camouflaged along with the winter clothes." Cy swiped to the photo of Joy's unconscious form, the last picture she had managed to take before the deputies kicked her out.

"How does that even happen?" asked Violet, frowning.

"She had one arm in a coat sleeve," said Cy. "She was probably in the middle of putting it on when she lost consciousness."

Violet threw her a skeptical glance.

"Well, here, let's experiment." Cy pulled Violet off the bed. "You're about the same height as Joy. Get your bathrobe." As Violet complied, Cy began piling clothes from the closet onto the cedar chest in the corner. Then Cy darted down the hall to her own room and brought back two pairs of moccasin slippers. "No, don't put the bathrobe on yet," she told Violet, then gave her one pair of slippers and instructed her to put those on; the other pair she placed at the base of the chest.

"So if I'm Joy," said Violet, "then I would've come over here…"

27

"That's right," said Cy as Violet moved to the end of the cedar chest.

"I put my boots on, then I started to put on my coat…" She put one arm into the sleeve of the bathrobe, then started with the other arm.

"Now fall over," Cy directed.

"Uh-huh. Sure." Starting with her knees, Violet endeavored to "fall" onto the chest without either hurting herself or moving her hands too far from their current position. In the end, she found her hands trapped under her body and her eyes staring down into the crack between the edge of the chest and the wall, one cheek against the clothing, the other pressed into the wallpaper.

Cy quickly snapped several photos from different angles, then told Violet to get up. They sat on the bed together and examined the images.

Violet grunted in amazement. "Son of a gun."

"You see?" Cy swiped back to the first photo. The clothes around Violet's head had fallen in, obscuring her from view, and among the other moccasins, the ones on Violet's feet looked jumbled with the others. A little of her calf showed, but Joy had been wearing boots that rose well past her ankles. The camouflage effect was total.

"So then what made her pass out?" wondered Violet.

"Probably something she ate or drank. It looks like they were close to finishing breakfast."

Violet looked again at the kitchen photos. She squinted. "Is that…eggs and toast?"

"M-maybe. I should've paid more attention when I was over there. Whatever they had, there's so little of it left, it's hard to tell."

"If it was eggs, that means one person probably made it for the other two."

Cy looked troubled. "Yeah, I guess so."

"That person could've put the drug in, and it took effect minutes after they ate it—after Kristy was upstairs and Joy was getting ready to leave."

"You're saying Fran did it?"

Violet shrugged.

Cy shook her head. "There's gotta be another possibility. What if... What if someone came early this morning—their footprints would be gone by now—and waited until the Dosleys were making breakfast. At some point when they weren't looking, that someone snuck in and messed with the food or the drinks. Then they went back into hiding and waited for the family to pass out. And then..." After a few seconds she deflated. "I don't know. I was going to say he kidnapped Fran or something, but..."

"But if your mother arrived soon after they finished breakfast, how could he have gotten away without her seeing?"

"Well, the same applies to Fran. How could *she* have gotten away without Mom noticing?"

"Do you think Fran's hidden somehow, the way Joy was?"

"Nah, by now they've turned that house inside out. If they'd found her, we'd have heard something."

Violet had been idly sliding the pictures across Cy's phone screen. She glanced down and saw an image of the Dosleys' backyard. Frowning, she said, "Does that back door go into the kitchen?"

"Yeah."

"Cy, look." She pointed to a bare patch of ground in the picture, just outside the back door. "That big tree is blocking the snow from piling up in this area. You could walk there and not leave footprints!"

"Yeah, but...as soon as you step out of it, you *do* leave footprints."

"Not if you went into the *woods*." Violet pointed to the closely grouped trees standing on the border of the yard.

Cy frowned, considering. "I guess. Thing is, if somebody went that way, dragging along an unconscious person, well, you'd think it'd look messier—more broken branches and stuff. Plus he couldn't have known my mom was gonna come over just then, so he wouldn't have planned to take her out that way. As soon as Mom showed up, he would've just left Fran and run."

"That's true."

"Anyway, if that's the way the poisoner went, he's long gone by now. It isn't that far to the town."

"Unless..." Violet looked up at Cy with wide eyes. "Unless he used the woods as cover to get to a nearby hiding place!"

"Where?"

"Here! He could've crept through the woods, come out behind this house, and—"

"Nope. Uh-uh. The poisoner's not hiding here, trust me."

"How do you know?"

"Because I went out the back door when I snuck over to take these photos. The only tracks by our back door are mine." She crawled across the bed to get to the window. "Look, you can still see—" She halted mid-speech, eyes riveted on the ground below. She put a hand to the glass. "Oh my god..."

"What? What is it?"

"Oh my god!" Cy leaped from the bed and charged out the door.

Violet scrambled to the window, looked down, and gasped.

Cy plowed through the kitchen, earning reprimands from both Rita and Deputy Hayden, which she ignored. She threw open the back door, darted outside, and shouted one more time, *"Oh my god!!"*

* * *

Jen felt as if the DePalmas' house wasted an awful lot of space. She knew this came partially from living in a large house that used its space efficiently; every one of its many rooms was no larger than it needed to be for its purpose. It was a house expressly for use, not for show. This house, though smaller than Jen's, looked large by normal standards, but once she passed through the front door she could see that the front half of the house consisted of one room, two stories high. A winding staircase off to the side gave access to a balcony that ran the width of the house; she could see the door of each room on the second floor from here. This house was meant for parties, for large groups of people to gather and see everyone else from anywhere.

In other words, this house belonged to rich people.

Thus, Jen was surprised at her first impression of the DePalmas. Most of the wealthier citizens she'd interacted with in the course of her career seemed pleased to see her; poorly did they hide their subconscious (or conscious) assumption that she, as a law officer, would act according to their will. Mr. and Mrs. DePalma, on the other hand, regarded her warily, like children with a substitute teacher—knowing anything they did might bring only disapproval.

Briefly, Jen fell under the impression that a party had indeed taken place recently, but no, it wasn't decorations and food littering the space. These were the normal items that tended to accumulate in any home over time when one wasn't expecting company, just spread over a larger area than she had ever seen. The first thing the occupants were about to say would be the usual, "Sorry about the mess."

Mr. DePalma closed the front door, turned to Jen, and said, "Just so we're clear, we're not taking the baby."

Although her training had helped it along, when she was a teenager, Jen had developed the ability to drain her face and voice, at will, of all emotion and expression. It was a handy way of getting out of trouble and made her a demon at poker. (She thanked the stars that the trait hadn't passed to Cy, that she'd always know what her daughter was feeling, even when she might not want to.) Nowadays Jen used it as a technique to elicit information.

Tilting her head to one side, she repeated, "The baby?" as if she'd never heard the term before.

"We heard Kristy's in the hospital because she ODed on drugs. You're gonna say she's an unfit mother and the baby has to come to us. We're not takin' it."

"We don't even know for sure Andy's the father," put in his wife. "This is proof the girl should've kept what happened to herself and put the baby up for adoption, instead of acting like she could take care of it."

Maintaining her neutral facade, which was also of benefit in that it masked the indignation building inside her, Jen said, "Is Andy here? I need to speak to him."

"Andy knows he doesn't have to take custody of the kid," rumbled Andy's father.

Jen fixed him with a stare and quietly repeated, "I need to speak with him."

Mr. DePalma might have continued to refuse, for all she knew, but his wife startled them both when she hollered, "Andy!"

toward one of the doors above the balcony. They waited, but there was no response. "Andy, you need to come down!" the woman yelled, slightly more shrilly. "It's the police!"

When still no movement or sound issued from upstairs, without a word Jen turned from the parents and marched up the steps. Andy's father dogged her while the mother trailed behind, wringing her hands and tittering something about her son being fatigued from his after-school job. Jen interrupted her by banging on Andy's door. "Andy, this is Deputy Grogan. Open the door now." She heard nothing. She felt the door; it was freezing cold. She opened it.

Across the room, beyond a sea of magazines and posters that seemed mainly to pertain to basketball, the window stood open, screen and all. There was no Andy.

There was hardness in her voice as Jen turned to the DePalmas and said, "I need to know where your son is."

"I'm sure he didn't run away just now," Mrs. DePalma protested. "He probably snuck out sometime last night—"

"Where is he?" Jen looked from one to the other of them, making sure they knew she'd run out of patience. "Where does he go when he sneaks out? To a friend's house?"

"Friends?" repeated Andy's father. "He doesn't have friends anymore! Not since it got around that he got a girl pregnant." As he ranted on, Jen scanned the bedroom for anything that might provide a clue to Andy's whereabouts. "Kristy's parents didn't even take her out of school when it happened! There were no consequences for her whatsoever! You gotta understand, our boy is not promiscuous, but that's what everyone assumed once it was clear Kristy's parents weren't punishing her at all. They acted like they had no shame. Now all the other parents think we *encouraged* Andy to sleep around!"

In a soft but bitter voice Mrs. DePalma said, "It's not fair for that girl to have a normal life while our boy's is ruined."

Completely normal, other than carrying a child, giving birth, and raising her, thought Jen. In as businesslike a tone as she could manage, she said, "I'm gonna need you to call your son."

Andy's father shook his head. "He won't answer. We'll just call you when he gets home."

Jen inhaled through her nose and kept her voice steady—just. "Sir, the mother of your grandchild didn't OD. Someone entered her home this morning and rendered her unconscious. One of her parents was knocked out the same way, and the other is missing. Now, apparently, so is your son." Both parents began to speak in protest, but she cut them off, "Either you call him right now or give me his number and I will." She could have alternated her glare between them, but instead she chose to focus it on the woman, betting that would achieve the desired result.

She was right. "Call the lawyer," Mrs. DePalma told her husband. "I'll call Andy." She pulled out her cell phone as Mr. DePalma strode off. Moments later Jen could hear Andy's phone ringing on the other end.

Then, with a frown, she pivoted. Something was also ringing inside this room. Digging through some pillows, she found a cell phone between the pages of a magazine on the bed.

"He left without his phone?!" His mother looked flummoxed. Jen handed the phone to her and ordered her to unlock it. The mother obeyed even as she muttered, "It won't matter. It won't tell you anything. He never calls anyone anymore."

A minute later, Jen showed her Andy's phone screen and said, "He's called this number at least a dozen times over the last few days. Whose is it?"

Mrs. DePalma was mystified. Jen proceeded to search through Andy's internet history.

She was barely into it before she gasped aloud, her mask of neutrality slipping entirely. A corner of her mind registered someone nearby saying, "What is it?" When Jen turned her head to look at Mrs. DePalma, her eyes bore such a look of accusation that the woman actually took a step back.

Jen swallowed, drew breath, spoke the word, "Wholesome," and then watched for the reaction.

Mrs. DePalma blinked. "Pardon?"

Jen doubted the woman was that good an actress. *So she doesn't know.*

As soon as she was out of the DePalmas' house, Jen contacted dispatch and had them put her through to Deputy Hayden. "Hayden," she said urgently, "Is the baby all right? Has her father shown up?"

Hayden reported that the baby was fine, and that the only newcomer had been Rosie's nanny. *"We were just about to call you,"* Hayden added. *"We just sent for another ambulance."*

Jen knew at once what the reason must be. "You found Fran?"

"Your daughter found her, actually. She was unconscious on your back porch."

"What?!!"

V

J en arrived home just in time to see Fran in a stretcher, being loaded into an ambulance in the Grogans' driveway. The morbidly humorous part of her brain conjured an image of the paramedics, prior to departing, asking her, "Before we go, are there any more? No? Are you sure?"

As one paramedic secured Fran, the other spoke to Jen. "She was struck on the back of the head with a blunt object. Blood trail shows she came out of the woods just behind your house and passed out on the back porch. She's heavily concussed."

"Well," said Jen, "she's probably got the same drug in her that knocked out—"

"No, the drug's not in her system."

"Say again?"

"I mean, of course we'll test for the drug, but I already know they won't find any."

"Why not?"

From inside the ambulance came a quite audible groan.

"If she'd been drugged, she wouldn't be able to do that, let alone manage locomotion."

"I see… Thank you."

The paramedic looked as if he were going to ask something, but then he seemed to change his mind.

* * *

"No, that's not how she was at all!"

"Cy, stay inside."

"I am inside!" Technically this was only half true, as Cy's upper body was leaning out an open kitchen window over the back porch.

"No offense to your kid," said Deputy Hayden, "but this is the exact spot where we found Fran Dosley."

"The spot, sure! But her arms and legs weren't all spread out like that. One of her arms was reached out farther than the other, and one leg was bent under her."

Jen, playing the part of the unconscious Fran, adjusted her limbs accordingly. "Like this?"

"Yeah, that's it."

Jen turned her head so she could see Deputy Hayden with one eye. "You concur?"

Hayden shrugged. "Maybe. First thing I did was check for a pulse. When I felt it, I turned her over and tried to revive her while Cy called the ambulance."

"That's exactly how she was!" called a voice. *"Just like that!"* The three of them craned their necks to see Violet leaning out her own window on the second floor.

"Please!" someone hissed behind Violet, who turned. The nanny, Rita, was leaning in through her doorway. "I just got the baby to sleep! You're going to wake her!"

"Sorry," Violet whispered.

Jen got to her feet. "So Fran was crawling," she murmured. "She was probably crawling all this time, all during our investigation, fading in and out of consciousness from her injuries."

"Through the woods?" Hayden said doubtfully.

"Then Violet was right," breathed Cy. "For some reason, Fran didn't get drugged like Joy and Kristy, so the poisoner attacked her. She ran away from him out the back door, and he chased her into the woods. They both ran across the spot where there isn't any snow, so neither of them left footprints. That must've been right before you went over there, Mom."

"I don't think so," said Hayden. "If the perp chased Fran out the back, he'd have had her at his mercy. She never would've made it this far. Something's off here."

Twigs crackled and snapped as Deputy Tan emerged from the woods at the back of the property, close to where a blood trail in the snow began, leading straight to the porch. "Blood traces run all the way over," Tan reported, "starting just behind the Dosley house."

"You see?" said Cy.

"Cy, close the window. Please," Jen added, hoping to convey that she was not annoyed but worried for her daughter's safety, given what she'd just realized.

Cy looked angry for an instant, then breathed through it, calmed herself, and obeyed.

"Hayden, stay here. But watch this door," Jen ordered. "Tan, with me."

The two deputies marched back to the Dosley property and stepped gingerly into the woods.

Violet's eyes followed them from her window as far as possible.

Tan noticed Jen's hand on her sidearm. "You think the perp's still nearby?" Tan asked quietly. "Wouldn't he or she have escaped back to town by now?"

"Maybe. But I think Fran put up more of a fight than he was expecting. I think the reason she made it all the way to my house is that he was hurt, too, and couldn't stop her."

"You keep saying, 'he.' Do you know who it was?"

"I know exactly who it was."

The ground was uneven in these woods, rising and falling sharply every few meters. The tree branches caught some of the snowfall, leaving large, white patches of ground here and there but plenty of bare spots where one could pass through without leaving footprints. The deputies followed these untouched sections of ground, heading in a general direction that led to town. Jen was no tracker, but she led her fellow deputy at a steady pace, as if guided by some strong instinct.

All at once they spotted movement, and they froze. Jen squinted, trying to peer past the ever-thickening shelves of snow on the tree branches.

"*Ssst.*" Tan waved, then shook her head and raised her hands in the shape of antlers, signifying it was a deer.

The ground was too covered with rocks, twigs, and leaves for them to have any hope of proceeding silently, so they wasted no effort sacrificing speed for stealth. The one compensation was the assurance that their quarry couldn't gain ground without them hearing *him* either.

Jen slowed her pace so as to fall back slightly, in step with Tan. "Don't stop walking," she said out of the corner of her mouth.

"I won't."

"You saw it?"

"Mm-hm."

Neither of them looked back at the boot wedged between some rocks.

Another few paces and Jen glimpsed an arm wrapped around a tree trunk. She thought it safe to assume Tan had seen it, too. "You left, me right."

"When?"

"Now."

They split apart without breaking pace. Only at the last second did they each dart forward, circling the target at five meters and stopping when at ninety degrees of each other, hands on sidearms. "Freeze!" Jen commanded.

The figure huddled at the base of the tree didn't move a muscle. Cautiously, the deputies drew nearer. One of the figure's feet lacked a boot. A winter hat lay on the ground nearby; his short brown hair was dusted with snow. He seemed to be holding his head close to the tree trunk, but closer up it looked as if he'd collapsed with his face pressed against the bark. "Jen," said Tan, "I think he's unconscious—"

"Wait!" Jen held out her hand. "He might be bluffing! Be careful."

Step by step they edged nearer.

"Andy DePalma?" Jen was close enough that she could see it was a teenage boy. "Andy, we're from the sheriff's department. If you can hear me, you need to say something now."

Tan squinted and ducked her head slightly. "Jen—he's bleeding."

"What?"

"His head's bleeding." She started forward.

"I said wait—"

With a cry, Andy opened his eyes and struggled to push himself up, startling the two deputies. He wavered, then lurched forward, trying to crawl away. Jen seized him and dragged him back. "No," he moaned. "No, I have to…have to stop her…"

"Andy DePalma," said Jen, taking out her handcuffs, "you're under arrest."

"I'm sorry…" Andy could barely keep his eyes open. "Shouldn't have… Shouldn't have… Have to stop her…"

"No, you don't. Kristy's not doing anything to you. She hasn't hurt you or shamed you. You did that, yourself." Jan slapped the handcuffs on.

"Jen, he's not a threat," Tan pointed out. "Are those really necessary?"

Jen gave her a look. Tan said nothing more, except to mention that they'd have to remember to read him his rights once he regained consciousness.

* * *

"Andy wanted to get out of his responsibilities as a father. As long as Rosie existed, that wasn't possible."

"He wasn't gonna *hurt* Rosie!?" Cy exclaimed.

"No, but he found a way to get her out of Veil, at least." Jen sighed as she leaned against the wall by Violet's bed, where Cy and Violet sat like pupils in a classroom. "He searched the internet and found a group called Wholesome—the page was still up on his phone when I checked it. It's a religious fundamentalist group whose main purpose is to tear apart families with same-sex parents."

"How is that legal?!" asked Violet.

"A lot of what they do isn't, but they keep that side of their activities hidden. They put up a front of using the system to 'achieve God's work' through legal channels. On paper they're all about marches and fundraisers for bills against gay marriage or adoption by gay couples, but in reality they use both sides of the law to push their homophobic agenda."

"But wait," said Cy, "Joy and Fran aren't lesbians. They're not even married. They're platonic co-parents."

Jen shrugged. "Either Andy didn't know that or he didn't tell Wholesome when he contacted them. Or maybe to them it's the same thing."

"Wait, he...*contacted* them?" Cy sounded appalled.

Jen nodded grimly. "I imagine to him it was the perfect opportunity. Wholesome takes Rosie away, illegally sells her to a new set of parents, and he doesn't have to feel ashamed anymore—and his parents no longer have to pay child support."

Cy and Violet glanced at each other but neither spoke. Both felt too sick.

"All he had to do," Jen went on, "was kidnap Rosie and deliver her to this group."

"So," said Violet, "he drugged Joy and Kristy, then had a fight with Fran outside?"

"That's right. They were both pretty banged up. He must've chased her out the back door into the woods. When they were done fighting, Fran started crawling this way and Andy crawled back toward—" She stopped, remembering...

She and Tan had found Andy collapsed against a tree, as if he'd been trying to crawl *past* it. Which would mean he'd been heading in the opposite direction from town—*toward* the Dosleys' house, not away from it.

Had she gotten something wrong...?

No. No, of course not, she assured herself, remembering the boot they'd found *between* Andy and the house. That proved he'd been heading toward town. He had to have lost the boot before he passed out. Hadn't he?

"Um, Mom?"

Jen shook herself. "Anyway, Andy's at the hospital under guard, Rita said she's fine taking care of Rosie until the Dosleys recover, and..." Her stomach chose that moment to growl. "I don't know about you two, but I clean forgot to have lunch."

Cy agreed, but Violet looked anything but enthusiastic about food.

"Cy," said Jen, noticing Violet's expression, "why don't you go tell Deputy Hayden she can go home. I'll be down in a minute to fix us something to eat."

"Okay."

Once Cy had left, Jen sat next to Violet on the bed. "You know, when they wake up, the Dosleys will probably want to thank you. You're the one who told me to go check on them."

Violet shifted uncomfortably. "You would've known something was wrong when Fran showed up on the back porch. Or the nanny would've found the others unconscious when she went to take care of Rosie."

"True. But thanks to you, Rosie had someone to take care of her that much sooner."

Violet nodded after a moment. "I guess."

"But you never really meant to send me over there, did you."

Violet blinked and her eyes went wide. "What?"

"I mean, you knew something was off with our neighbors today, but you hadn't given it that much thought. It was just what you said at the time to divert the conversation from what was *really* bothering you. I'm a detective, remember?" she said in response to Violet's astonished stare. "So…do you want to talk about it?"

Twice Violet opened her mouth to speak, but, try as she might, she could not make any sound come out.

"It's about Marcy, isn't it," Jen said gently. "The feelings are so strong, you think they're gonna crush you if you say them out loud."

Eyes on the floor, Violet nodded, her jaw trembling.

Jen swallowed, took a deep breath. "I'm going to say something. If you want me to stop, I will. I think you're imagining Marcy's death over and over."

Violet's mouth dropped open to form a small O.

"I think you're picturing it again and again in your head, trying to calculate out how much she suffered. What happened to her is too horrible to contemplate, so you're desperate to reassure yourself it wasn't that bad. You keep hoping that if you think about it hard enough, it'll be all right. But deep down, you know it won't."

Violet wiped away a tear and, sniffling, nodded in amazement. "That's it exactly. I've been trying and trying not to think about it. I don't *want* to think about it. No matter how it happened... Sh-she must've been so afraid. But when I try to stop thinking about it, I feel guilty—like I'm leaving her to die alone. I just can't imagine—being scared, helpless, someone's hands grabbing her, trapping her as she tried to get away, snapping her neck..."

Jen grasped Violet's hand. "You can stop now."

Violet turned pleading eyes on her. "I don't know how."

"The coroner's report shows Marcy was knocked unconscious by a blow from behind before she died. She never knew what was about to happen. She didn't suffer."

It took a few seconds before the dam broke. As Violet wept in her arms, Jen stroked her hair and shushed her soothingly. "I know," she whispered. "We're all grieving for her. Shh."

* * *

"Deputy! She's coming to!"

"Ms. Dosley? Ms. Dosley, it's all right. You were injured, but you're in the hospital. You're going to be fine. I'm Deputy Derrick. We know you and your family were attacked, but don't worry. Your wife and daughter are also here in the hospital getting care, and your nanny is taking care of the baby. Everything's going to be fine...Ms. Dosley? Nurse! I think she blacked out again."

***

Jen poured herself a glass of water from the kitchen sink and had drunk most of it before her phone rang. "Grogan."

"Grogan, it's Derrick. I'm at the hospital. We have a problem."

"What is it?"

"The doctors say Andy DePalma received his injuries long before Fran received hers. We're talking at least an hour."

For a moment Jen did nothing, then she set the glass down firmly on the counter. "That's impossible."

"Doctors are pretty sure. And we know there wasn't anyone else in that house. It must've been Joy or Kristy who attacked Fran."

No, thought Jen. *I don't believe it.* There must have been someone else—but how? If that someone else had exited through the back of the house, they would've prevented Fran from reaching next door. If they'd left by the front, they would've left footprints—unless...

Could they have gone out the front...and gotten away by stepping in the footprints left by Jen, herself? But wait, that would mean—

"Pardon? She is? Grogan, Fran's awake—barely. Seems like she's anxious to say something."

Jen heard some faint, confused noises on the other end, then a choppy gust of breath from a mouth held close to the phone, followed by a desperate, raspy voice: *"We—don't—have—a nanny!"*

VI

"I'm feeling better," said Violet. She used a tissue to dry her eyes; it was the last tissue in the box. "I owe you guys, like, ten boxes of tissues."

"Don't worry, I'll put it on your tab."

Violet blinked. "I have a tab?"

"No!" Cy swatted her with a pillow. "Stop worrying about what you owe us."

"No promises."

"Whatever. Come down and have some lunch."

"Is the baby down there? I don't want to get the baby sick."

"I told you, you're not contagious anymore! Plus, the baby's asleep in Mom's room. Oh my god!"

"What?"

"You never drank the Tang I made you!" She pointed at the glass of Tang sitting on the windowsill.

Violet grimaced. "I'm actually not too fond of Tang. The taste is kind of...tangy."

"I gave you, like, twenty glasses of it while you were sick!"

"Yeah, when you're sick, you can't taste much."

"Oh, for Pete's sake. I'll drink it, then." Cy circled the foot of the bed toward the window. "What do you want to drink, then? Milk? Soda? Iced tea?"

Violet was halfway to the door when she froze. *Tea... Milk... Tang... Holy—*

She whipped around. "No, Cy, don't!"

* * *

Jen heard movement behind her. She spun around, and as she did so, her phone slipped from her hand and fell to the floor. Vaguely she wondered why she'd dropped it... Clumsy...

Rita was packing the baby equipment into her canvas bag. Rita... Who was she again? She was...the nanny! The *fake* nanny! The impostor! Jen reached for her sidearm.

"Did you see where the other formula bottle went?" asked Rita. "Oh, wait, I remember." She retrieved the bottle from the fridge.

"You..." Why was it getting difficult to speak? "You're with... Wholesome."

"Hm? Oh, yes," said Rita mildly.

Jen took out her handcuffs. "You're under arr..." She was so busy trying to remember the second syllable that she didn't notice her legs falling out from under her. It wasn't until her elbow painfully struck the bench beside the kitchen table that she began to have an inkling of what was happening. Her drooping eyes picked out her unfinished glass of water on the counter. She sputtered, "D-drugged..."

"Yes, I brought a second kit just in case something went wrong with the first one. I always say redundancy is a wise precaution, no matter how cumbersome it might be."

Somehow, despite the loss of feeling in her limbs, Jen managed to draw her sidearm.

"Now, now," chided Rita, deftly relieving Jen of the weapon, "let's not have loaded guns near infants." As she removed the bullets and finished packing, she went on, "Now, I'd say I have just enough time to leave with Rosie before your compatriots return—although, having thought about it the last few hours, I've decided 'Mary' would suit her much better. There aren't nearly enough Marys these days, don't you think?" She strode past Jen and began to head up the stairs—and felt something clamp around her ankle. She turned back to find the deputy clutching her, her lips pulled back, teeth gritted. "My goodness," Rita exclaimed. "It's taking longer than usual with this one." She batted at Jen's hand, felt the fingers around her ankle squeeze harder. "Oh, dearie me." Rita drew back her fist and drove it into Jen's face. The deputy flopped on the bottom steps like a rag doll, completely senseless, blood trickling from over her eye. "That's better," Rita sighed. She marched primly up the stairs, leaving Jen sprawled below.

"Ro-sie," Rita cooed as she headed down the hall toward the bedroom where she'd left the infant asleep. "Time for us to go." She stepped into the room.

Rosie was not in the nest of blankets on the bed where Rita had left her.

Rita stepped back and drew a slow, silent breath and listened intently as she pivoted. Every door in this hallway was closed… except one. Rita quietly retraced her steps toward the back staircase, approaching the bedroom closest to it. She leaned her head through the door. Inside, sprawled facedown, lay the teenage girl, Cy. A spilt glass of Tang stained the floor nearby.

Rita turned back to face the hall full of doors. Closing her eyes, she padded carefully down the hall, concentrating, tuning her ears to pick up the slightest noise. She'd made it to the front staircase at the end of the hall before she heard something— some small movement from the alcove just beside the top of the stairs. Could someone be hiding there? It didn't seem large enough for a full-grown person to hide, but Rita hadn't heard a sound from anywhere else—

Behind her, a door opened. Rita darted behind the open door of the bedroom where she'd last seen the baby. Violet, wearing a face mask, peeked out of the room next door. Seeing no one, she crept into the hall and, carrying the sleeping baby, made her way toward the back staircase.

"I wouldn't go down those stairs."

Violet gasped and halted. She turned around and saw Rita standing at the opposite end of the hall.

"You see," said Rita, pacing slowly forward, "there's a body cluttering the bottom of the stairs. Very difficult to step over while holding an infant. You could lose your grip."

"Please," said Violet in as even a voice as she could muster. "Just leave. There are no more deputies. You could make a clean getaway."

Rita shook her head with an amused smile. "I've never hurt a child," she said, "and I'm not about to start now."

Violet gave her an incredulous look. "You think it's *hurting* her to let her stay with her family?!"

The humor left Rita's face. "Those people are not fit to be her family. *Anyone's* family." She held out her arms, getting nearer and nearer. "Now, give her to me. I promise to find her a real home, to be raised by good parents...who aren't perverted or promiscuous."

Trembling, Violet began to back away. "You're a monster."

"I am a savior of children. With the power given to me by the grace of God, I will not let delinquents pass on their depravity to another generation."

Violet's trembling turned from fear to fury. She stopped backing away and took a defiant stance. "No. You're no savior.

49

You're a judgy bitch. And I will never let you touch this baby."

Rita stopped a few feet away from her and gave her a pitying smile. "And who are you to stop me?"

"I'm not. He is." Violet nodded at someone behind Rita.

Rita knew she had not heard a man's tread behind her. "Bluffing won't help you," she said.

But then she *did* hear something. It started out low, then got louder and higher in pitch. It sounded like a wasp buzzing, but it was more guttural. Almost like a cat, but no cat could ever sound like—

Rita whipped around and saw Roswell crouched at her feet, teeth bared, ears flattened, hackles raised—and then he shot forward, triggered by Rita's sudden movement, and sank his claws and teeth into her leg.

Violet dashed into the nearest spare bedroom, knowing she had mere seconds. The baby, hearing Rita's cries and Roswell's snarls, had started to wake up. "Please don't say anything," Violet whispered.

Rita managed to shake off the cat, then shoved him into Cy's room and slammed the door. With a speed and agility no one would've thought her capable of, she zipped down to the door Violet had gone through and glimpsed Violet slipping into the connecting bathroom. Rita darted back to where the bathroom opened up into the hall and threw open the door, only to find that Violet had doubled back and was making for the back staircase. Rather than head down and risk dropping her precious bundle while stepping over Jen's prone form, Violet headed up to the third floor. Rita reached the stairs just as Violet got to the top, and she tore after her.

There were only three rooms on the top floor, all of them empty. Rita paused at the top of the stairs; she wasn't about to enter one room only to have Violet slip out of another one and make it past her back down to the lower floors. She held her breath so that she might hear Violet's, but she detected nothing. Cautiously she stepped further into the open space, equidistant from the three doors. She shifted from side to side, trying to spot Violet or her shadow. Could she risk leaning her head in to check each of the rooms one by one, while still keeping an eye on the other two? With her focus divided, she might fall victim to an ambush.

This was taking too long. Rita lifted her foot and stomped down hard. A startled "Oh!" escaped from the room on the left.

Rita entered to find Violet backed into the corner, clutching Rosie in her blanket as before. The older woman shook her head admonishingly. "If you're sick enough to have to wear a mask, you shouldn't be holding an infant, let alone running with one."

With the mask concealing most of Violet's face, all that could be seen were her eyes. Those eyes looked from the baby to Rita. There was fierceness in those eyes as she spoke quietly. "You think I'm afraid to risk injuring her?" She took an aggressive step toward Rita. "You just assume I'd rather give her to you than risk her getting hurt?" She took another step.

"No more bluffing," Rita ordered. "Just hand her over."

"Maybe *you're* the one who's bluffing," Violet countered, stepping closer. "If you really care so much, you'll let me walk by you without trying to take her from me. I could lose my grip, remember?"

She took half a step toward the narrow space between Rita and the door—and Rita slammed her hand against the wall, blocking her way. Rita hissed, "One way or another, I am not letting that child be raised by those f—"

"Don't you *dare* use that word where she can hear you!" Violet was getting closer, her eyes blazing with fury. "You really want her that badly? You want her?!"

"Calm down—"

"You really want her?! *HERE!*"

She threw the baby.

Rita yelped as she fumbled to catch the bundle. To her horror, as she caught the edge of the blanket between her fingers, it unrolled, letting its contents fall, spinning, to the floor...

A hair dryer clattered noisily.

Rita looked up at Violet—

—and glimpsed her top half just before Violet slid down the laundry chute.

Violet tried to use her legs to slow down her momentum as she shot toward the second-floor laundry room. Still, she landed painfully at the bottom. Muttering, "Ow, ow, ow," she grabbed a clean towel, charged down the hall, collected Rosie from where she'd left her in the spare bedroom, and shot toward the front staircase.

She was halfway down, mere feet from the front door, when she heard glass shattering from above, followed by a THUMP on the roof over the front of the house. "What the—?" Next, just outside the front window, something whizzed downward and landed in the thick snow.

Violet hesitated. Perhaps a leg had been broken—no one could dive down three stories, one after another in quick succession, and still be walking.

Rita rose out of the snow like a vampire from a coffin and stared Violet straight in the eye.

Violet bolted. She had to get out of this house. She had no boots on, but Rosie's safety was worth a pair of soaking, freezing feet. Holding the baby to her chest, she skittered past the stairs, through the dining room and into the kitchen, knocking over chairs and whatever else she could along the way to slow Rita's pursuit—

And found herself facing Rita as the woman entered through the back door. She was covered with snow, and wheezing; she'd sprinted all the way around the house to cut Violet off. But she was in no way winded. She stalked toward Violet, eyeing her menacingly, lips pulled back, sucking in air through her teeth.

Violet, backing away and nearly tripping over Jen's leg, put a hand to the wall to steady herself. Frantically she tried to think of a way out but was unable to look away from that flushed, furious face.

Rita drew a deep breath. "Now…give—me—the b—"

Violet's hand, moving along the wall, found a doorknob. She twisted it and flung the door open, nailing Rita dead in the face.

Amid the ensuing bellows of agony, Violet considered her options: Jen's body was blocking the stairs, and the way back was littered with bulky odds and ends that Violet had upended.

From the other side of the door, Rita heard Violet's footsteps descending to the basement. Thrusting the door aside, she followed.

The staircase ran alongside one wall of the basement. There was no other exit. For Violet, there was nowhere left to run. Rather than squeeze into the farthest corner, Violet had taken a few steps from the stairs, then turned about to face Rita as she came down. She was breathing fast, clearly scared but trying to keep control of herself.

Rita wiped blood from her lip. "I have to admit I'm impressed…but when it comes down to whose will is greatest, there's never any contest. God always triumphs over evil."

Violet stood there, unmoving, not looking about for a place to hide, just keeping her eyes fixed on Rita's. Only when Rita reached out with both arms did Violet step sideways, away from the wall—still maintaining eye contact. Slowly, mechanically, they moved across the concrete floor, one forward, one backward. Inevitably they reached another wall, and both stopped.

Rosie squirmed in Violet's arms, gurgling.

Rita reached toward the baby, and Violet offered no resistance. Neutrally she stared into Rita's eyes—and finally it occurred to Rita to wonder why she was doing that. Why wasn't she looking anywhere else, in desperation? For a dark corner to hide in? For a weapon, amongst these boxes and dusty tool chests, to use in self-defense? For a way to get back to the staircase, which, given how Violet had led her, was now directly behind Rita—

"*FREEZE!!!*"

Rita turned—and gave a jolt of surprise to see Cy standing, wide awake, on the lower part of the stairs, pointing a weapon directly at her.

"Don't move or I'll shoot," Cy warned.

Hearing Violet shuffle away from her, and despite her still-hurting mouth, Rita smiled. "You would never fire a gun near an infant."

She took a step toward Violet.

Cy fired.

With a choked gasp, Rita convulsed, much more of her hurting now than just her face. Within seconds she lay spread-eagled on the floor, insensate, her limbs still jerking.

Violet leaned her head back in relief and gratitude.

Cy, too, let out a sigh of relief. "Gun, no," she said. "Taser, yes."

VII

"Jen?" said a voice.

Something began to take shape before Jen's eyes.

"Hey, Jen, can you hear me?"

The shape got bigger. Closer. A head. A face. "Wh-whozat?"

"It's Violet."

"Violet..." The shape started to resolve. Jen made out a pair of green eyes, two cheeks and a nose all covered in freckles, black hair with a purple bow...a beautiful smile...

A trickle of blood running down the center of her forehead—

Gasping, she tried to sit up. "Violet!!"

Her movement seemed to make the image swim and distort. She felt a gentle hand on her arm. "Whoa, take it slow, okay? You've been out for six hours." The image slowed and resolved again, this time into a face with amber eyes, no freckles, and dark brown hair, *sans* bow. Behind the face were the bright fluorescent lights and greenish-white walls of the Veil hospital.

Jen shut her eyes tight and groaned. "Where's Cy?"

"She's helping change Rosie. She'll be back in a minute."

After a series of successive winces and eye-rubbings, Jen woke herself up enough to process her surroundings: she was in a small hospital room with an IV attached to her arm. She was still in her deputy's uniform, with the sleeve rolled up.

"Do you remember what happened?" asked Violet.

As Jen tried to concentrate, she felt a dull ache above her left eye. She pictured Rita's fist sailing toward her. "Rita," she said groggily, "the nanny...she's from Wholesome."

Violet nodded. "Yeah. She's at the sheriff's station now. In a jail cell."

Not quite taking in all that she heard, Jen half-rose. "She's gonna kidnap Rosie!"

"Rosie's fine!" Violet assured her, easing her back down. "The doctors checked her over and she's okay. She's with Kristy."

"Kristy's awake?"

"They all are. They've been talking our ears off—well, Joy has. Fran's a little quieter. Joy told me she has an open part-time position at her store. So I guess I've got a job now!" She smiled excitedly, then quickly sobered. "I can pay rent if you want."

"You're awake!" Cy barreled in through the door and gave her mother a quick hug. Then she stood back and folded her arms. "What's the point of keeping a taser in your bedroom if it's at the back of the bottom dresser drawer? It took me forever to find it!"

Grunting and groaning, Jen pushed herself to a sitting position and gave her head several little shakes. Brushing aside offers of help from Cy and Violet, she regarded them both steadily. "So you two took down the nanny."

Cy shrugged in a poor attempt at modesty. Violet looked down, blushing.

"But how did you know Rita was...?"

"We saw her—attack you," said Cy. "We were at the top of the stairs."

Jen nodded, unconsciously bringing her hand to where Rita had struck her. There was probably a bruise under the bandage.

"The nurse said you don't have any broken bones," Violet told her. "It was mainly the drug in your system that knocked you out."

"That's right, she drugged me... How did she drug me? For that matter, how did she drug the Dosleys? I thought it was Andy."

A look passed between Cy and Violet. The latter said, "Sheriff Dubowski came and talked to the Dosleys a little while ago. When Andy woke up, he confessed that he'd contacted Wholesome and asked them to take Rosie away."

"But then he grew a conscience," said Cy, "and he went out and tried to stop the kidnapping. He should've called the Dosleys and warned them, or called the sheriff, but he didn't want anyone to know what he'd done. He confronted Rita early in the morning, in the woods behind the Dosley house. When she wouldn't back down, he *was* going to call the sheriff or the Dosleys, but she knocked him out."

"So that's why Andy was knocked out first," Jen mused. She could picture him losing his boot as he ran from Rita toward town, then, after she'd downed him, he started back toward the Dosleys' to try to "stop her," as he'd tried to say.

Cy continued, "Rita broke into the Dosleys' before they woke up and rigged this—this—I don't know what to call it—this equipment under the kitchen sink, hooking it up to their pipes so it would contaminate the faucet water with the knockout drug."

A kit, Jen remembered Rita had called it. "But if it was still there, under the sink, why didn't Derrick and the other deputies find it when they searched the house?"

Again Cy and Violet exchanged glances, this time more uncomfortably. Violet cleared her throat. "We, um, overheard the sheriff...chastising Deputy Derrick for not looking under the kitchen sink."

"Why wouldn't he have looked there?"

Cy screwed up her face, trying to remember. "Something about Deputy Tan and dead bodies being stuffed into small spaces."

Jan looked at Violet, who shook her head quickly. "It's not worth repeating. Anyway, the Dosleys woke up, they had breakfast, and Joy and Kristy passed out."

"Why not Fran?"

"Because she didn't drink any water. Rita came in to abduct the baby, expecting all the adults to be out cold. Fran surprised her, and they ended up having a fight outside. Rita won the fight and came back in for the baby..."

"But that's right when you came to the house," Cy took over. "She knew you were going to send for reinforcements and search everywhere, so she snuck over to our house by—"

"Stepping in my footprints," Jen supplied, nodding.

Cy gave a slight pout. "Okay, I was kinda proud of myself for figuring that part out, but whatever."

Jen went on, "And then she hid in our house until she pretended to arrive, posing as the nanny."

"But," put in Violet, "before she came out of hiding, she contaminated our—your house's water system the same way."

Jen gave her a look of reproach. "You can say, 'our' house, Violet. It's okay."

Violet nodded with a bashful smile. "I'll work on that."

"It's lucky neither of you drank any of the water."

"Oh, I almost did," said Cy. "Violet stopped me just in time. But I pretended I'd drunk it so I'd have a chance to find the taser and get the jump on Rita."

When Jen looked inquiringly at her, Violet explained, "I remembered that, in the photos Cy showed me—the ones she took in the Dosley house—the three drinks on the breakfast table were tea, Tang, and milk. I realized that's why only two of the Dosleys got drugged—because two ingested water and one didn't. I didn't know how the drug was introduced into the water, so I figured there might be something wrong with…with our water, too."

"The sheriff's got people fixing the water in both houses," Cy informed her mother.

Jen let out a long breath and leaned back, looking proudly at them both. To Violet she said, "All this because you were worried about our neighbors being too quiet."

Violet opened her mouth to speak.

Cy pointed at her. *"Don't* say you didn't do anything."

Violet rolled her eyes, but she was smiling. "I was going to say, it felt really good helping those people, and I was wondering… barring any unforeseen circumstances…whether I might be able to train to become a deputy."

She looked uncertainly at Jen, who finally nodded. "I think we can look into that."

Cy and Violet exchanged grins.

"After all, we can't let Deputy Benno be the rookie in the group forever."

* * *

THREE DAYS LATER

Benno sulked as he trudged toward his car—his personal car, not one of the patrol vehicles. It was small and had no trunk to speak of, but since Benno had moved to Veil, he hadn't needed anything larger.

He'd discovered two, possibly three more deaths in Vermont

that contained what could be allusions, however slight, to "Pop Goes the Weasel," but the sheriff would still hear none of it. Not until some form of physical evidence linked the deaths. Benno was growing anxious. His gut told him these were murders, all committed by one party. They stretched back more than two years; what if they'd been going on for even longer? And who would be the next victim? This killer had been at work without drawing suspicion for so long. He could strike anywhere, anytime.

Benno got into his car without looking in the back seat.

What confused him the most was why the killer would leave clues pertaining to the song if he didn't want the string of murders to be recognized as such. Was that why he made it plain what had happened to Marcy Temple? So that someone would draw the connection between the pepper on her nose and the other clues? Benno had to admit there was some logic in it. Start killing people off and you're likely to be caught before you get very far in terms of a body count. But hide the fact that anyone's been murdered, wait until you've killed a large number of people, and *then* tip off the authorities as to what you've been doing... *That* would achieve notoriety, or infamy, if something of that nature was what the killer was after. A song such as "Pop Goes the Weasel," with most of its lyrics not well known, was the perfect device for such a purpose.

But it hadn't worked. The sheriff hadn't bought the theory. The clues had been too subtle. If the killer wanted credit for his work, he'd have to do something more blatant, more explicit—like claiming another victim. Or victims. And there was nothing anyone could do about it.

Benno inhaled through his nose and sighed heavily, his eyes shut.

Then he opened his eyes and frowned. He sniffed again. He made a face. He turned in his seat—

With a strangled cry he fumbled at the door handle, got it on the third try, and tumbled out of his car. He scrambled to his feet and, with shaking hands, took out his phone and activated the flashlight.

Two figures occupied the back seat of his car. Benno swallowed, fighting back nausea as the light found two pairs of glossy eyes staring out of decaying flesh. One head was misshapen, with rust-colored pieces flaking off and embedding themselves in the car's upholstery. The other seemed to be staring at the bullet hole in its chest.

There was something just below the bullet hole. Benno had no desire to get closer, but he did, holding the phone with both hands to stop the light from shaking so much.

A sign hung from Rob Mulroy's neck, the cardboard resting on his belly. It read, *WEASEL*.

Benno shifted. Another sign adorned Matt Foley's corpse: *MONKEY*.

From nearby Benno heard someone whistling the notes of a familiar song. He spun around, sweeping the area with his phone light, but it wasn't bright enough to penetrate all the shadows. "Who's there?!" Benno shouted. "Who are you??!"

He got no answer.

WINTER IN VEIL

A Mystery Novella Series
by Miles Ledoux

Next time in Veil...

Swallowing, Violet said, "I have to go on the trail. If I find the spot where I saw this symbol, the rest of the memory might come back." She felt a tear running down her cheek. Frantically she brushed it away.

"But, sir," protested Benno, "we shouldn't be forcing Violet, as a witness, to go through something traumatic—"

"It's more than that," Violet said in a loud voice, before the sheriff could reply. "It's not just about me being a witness. Think about it." To herself, she added in a low voice, "I *have* to go."

Benno glanced at Jen, nonplussed. "I don't understand."

Violet looked at him. "I haven't left Veil since I woke up here. I haven't gone on any camping trail. The only way I could have a memory from there... The reason I'm having so much trouble remembering it clearly...is if it happened *before* my amnesia."

Jen, Benno, and the sheriff shared a collective shiver.

"If it really was the serial killer in that memory...then it's possible..." Violet ran her fingers over her scar. Her hand was shaking. "He's the one who did this to me. He's the reason I can't remember."

"POP! GOES THE WEASEL"

All around the cobbler's bench
   The monkey chased the weasel
   The monkey thought 'twas all in fun
   Pop! goes the weasel
   Queen Victoria's very sick
   Prince Albert has the measles
   The children have the whooping cough
   Pop! goes the weasel

You may try to sew and sew
   And never make anything regal
   Roll it up and let it go
   Pop! goes the weasel
   A penny for a spool of thread
   A penny for a needle
   That's the way the money goes
   Pop! goes the weasel

A painter would his lover to paint
   He stood before the easel
   The monkey jumped all over the paint
   Pop! goes the weasel

When his sweetheart, she did laugh
His temper got so lethal
He tore the painting up in half
Pop! goes the weasel

My son and I went to the fair
We saw a lot of people
We spent a lot of money there
Pop! goes the weasel
I got sick from all the sun
My boy, he got the measles
Still, we had a lot of fun
Pop! goes the weasel

I climbed up and down the coast
To find a golden eagle
I climbed the rocks and thought I was close
Pop! goes the weasel
But, alas, I lost my way
Saw nothing but a seagull
I tore my pants and killed the day
Pop! goes the weasel

I went to the grocery store
I thought a little cheese'll
Be 'nough to catch a mouse on the floor
Pop! goes the weasel
But the mouse was very bright
He wasn't a mouse to wheedle
He took the cheese and said, "Goodnight!"
Pop! goes the weasel

Half a pint of twopenny rice
  Half a pint of treacle
  Mix it up and make it nice
  Pop! goes the weasel
  Up and down the London road
  In and out of the Eagle
  That's the way the money goes
  Pop! goes the weasel

Ev'ry night when I go out
  The monkey's on the table
  Take a stick and knock it off
  Pop! goes the weasel
  Put some pepper on his nose
  And you'll make him sneeze-l
  Catch him fast before he snaps
  Pop! goes the weasel

If you want to buy a pig
  Buy a pig with hairs on
  Every hair a penny a pair
  Pop! goes the weasel
  A penny for a cotton ball
  A penny for a needle
  That's the way the money goes
  Pop! goes the weasel

All around the cobbler's bench
  The monkey chased the weasel
  The monkey thought 'twas all in fun
  Pop! goes the weasel

66

I've no time to wait and sigh
I've no time to tease-l
Kiss me quick, I'm off, goodbye...

About the Author

Miles Ledoux was born in upstate New York and started writing murder mysteries at the age of nine. His first paid writing gig was in 2007, when a local theatre chose one of his plays for their summer melodrama. He received other royalties after moving to Los Angeles for graduate school, where he wrote, directed, and produced several mystery dessert theatre plays. He also started a side business designing and running mystery party games while working as a martial arts instructor.

Currently the author resides in Springfield, Vermont. Despite having lived in five different states, he has remained active in community theatre as a playwright, director, and actor. He also has a YouTube channel where he compares Agatha Christie adaptations to the books they were based on. His handle is @MysteryMiles.

Miles loves books, cats, music, Star Trek, Peanuts, and owns an ever-growing number of variations of the board game Clue. His favorite author is Lloyd Alexander.

You can connect with me on:

🌐 https://www.ledouxmysteries.com

www.ingramcontent.com/pod-product-compliance
Lightning Source LLC
Chambersburg PA
CBHW071345130626
46556CB00005B/2037